IRRADIATED BY COSMIC RAYS AND TRANSFORMED TO POSSESS SUPERHUMAN POWERS, THEY JOINED TOGETHER TO FIGHT EVIL. **MISTER FANTASTIC,** THE **INVISIBLE WOMAN,** THE **HUMAN TORCH** AND THE **THING.** TOGETHER THEY CALL THEMSELVES THE FANTASTIC FOUR IN

WOMEN ARE FROM VENUS, MEN ARE FROM ATLANTIS

JEFF PARKER WRITER
MANUEL GARCIA PENCILS
SCOTT KOBLISH INKS
SOTOCOLOR'S A. CROSSLEY COLORS
DAVE SHARPE LETTERS
PAGULAYAN, HUET and SOTOMAYOR COVER
JACOB CHABOT PRODUCTION
NATHAN COSBY ASST. EDITOR
MARK PANICCIA EDITOR
MACKENZIE CADENHEAD CONSULTING EDITOR
JOE QUESADA CHIEF
DAN BUCKLEY PUBLISHER

MARVEL
Spotlight

VISIT US AT
www.abdopublishing.com

Spotlight library bound edition © 2007. Spotlight is a division of ABDO Publishing Company, Edina, Minnesota.

Cataloging Data

Parker, Jeff

Fantastic Four in women are from Venus, men are from Atlantis / Jeff Parker, writer ; Manuel Garcia, pencils ; Scott Koblish, inks. -- Library bound ed.

p. cm. -- (Fantastic Four)

Summary: Irradiated by cosmic rays and transformed to possess superhuman powers, Mr. Fantastic, the Invisible Woman, the Human Torch, and the Thing join together to fight evil.

"Marvel age"--Cover.

Revision of the February 2006 issue of Marvel adventures Fantastic Four.

ISBN-13: 978-1-59961-206-5

ISBN-10: 1-59961-206-2

1. Fantastic Four (Fictitious characters)--Comic books, strips, etc.--Fiction. 2. Graphic novels. I. Title. II. Title: Women are from Venus, men are from Atlantis III. Series.

741.5dc22

All Spotlight books are reinforced library binding
and manufactured in the United States of America

Umm... faster, maybe?
I'm *trying*.
I'm *sure* that's one of the Imperial Guardfish written of in legends! That means we're close to the fabled underwater city of Atlantis!
No, it means we're close to being a Fantastic Four-Course Dinner!

It's got us!
What speed! It closed the distance in a second!
Do we have a weapon to fire? Reed?
Sue Storm to Reed Richards, over!
Oh, wow. This glass can withstand 100 fathoms of pressure and that fish's bite is still cracking it.
Stop being impressed by the thing that's eating us!
Everyone--helmets on *now!*
You too!
CRUNCH
Ahh! We're toast!
No, I've got us in a force field--open your eyes!
Now everyone be quiet.
Nice, sis! The fish can't see us!
Shhh! A big part of being invisible is *being quiet,* Johnny.

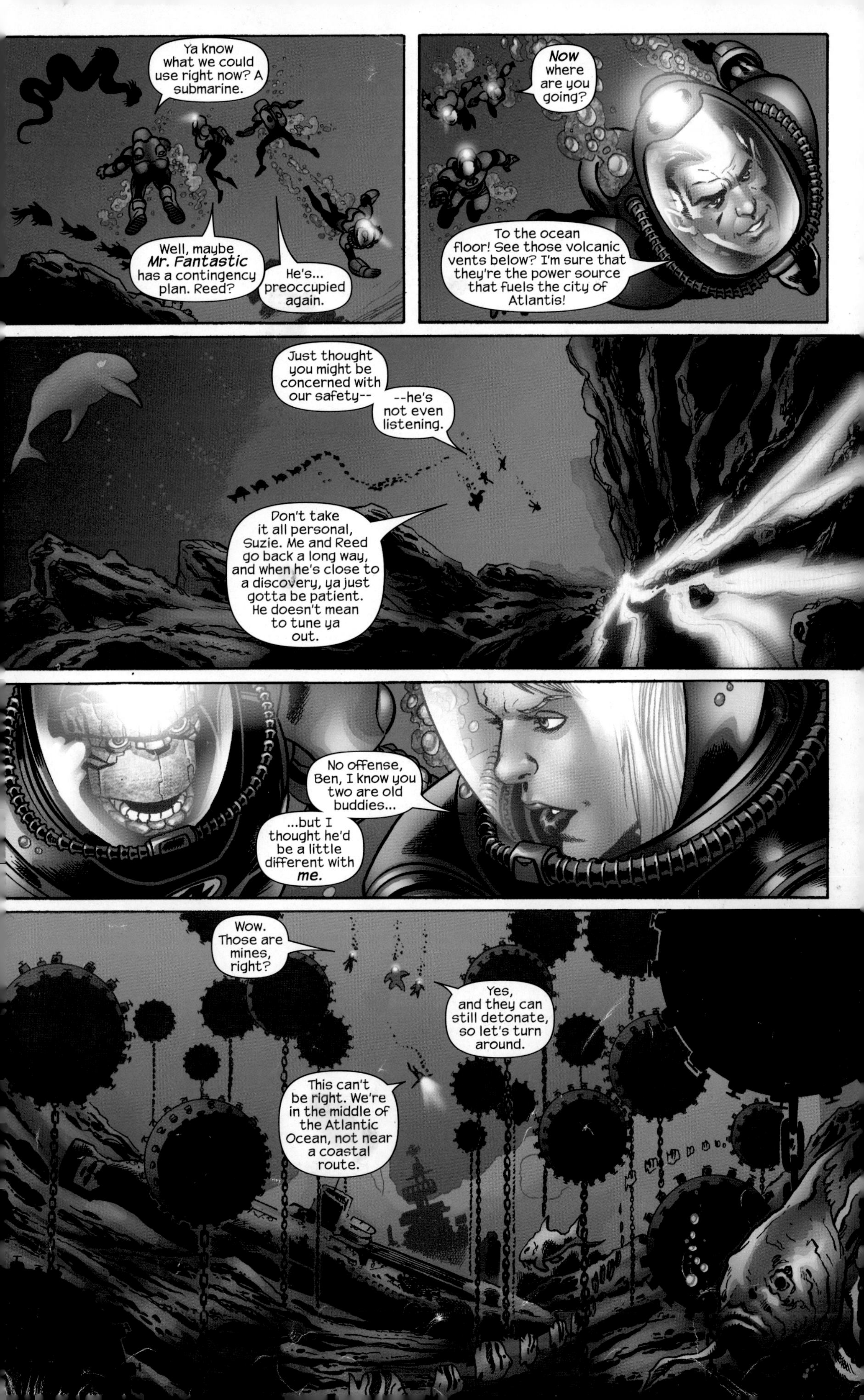
Ya know what we could use right now? A submarine.
Well, maybe Mr. Fantastic has a contingency plan. Reed?
He's... preoccupied again.
Now where are you going?
To the ocean floor! See those volcanic vents below? I'm sure that they're the power source that fuels the city of Atlantis!
Just thought you might be concerned with our safety--
--he's not even listening.
Don't take it all personal, Suzie. Me and Reed go back a long way, and when he's close to a discovery, ya just gotta be patient. He doesn't mean to tune ya out.
No offense, Ben, I know you two are old buddies...
...but I thought he'd be a little different with me.
Wow. Those are mines, right?
Yes, and they can still detonate, so let's turn around.
This can't be right. We're in the middle of the Atlantic Ocean, not near a coastal route.

Ben, you're a World War II buff--were any major sea battles fought around here?
Come ta think of it... no. But I'm no expert.
I trust your knowledge.
Reed, no!
STOP!
Are you in-
-sane?
Good holograms, they even appear to sway with the current.
Come on through, you have to see...
...Atlantis.

Okay... you were right.
Do we go knock? Ask fer a cup 'a sugar?
Yes! This is an opportunity for information exchange! Look at the technology they must have--imagine all the lost history they know!
Just imagine...
--a big sea serpent? Because that's what I'm imagini--
ZZAATTZZZAATTTZZZAATT
--NG!
Actually young man, she's a giant eel. A giant electric eel.
Bring them to the royal chambers.

Ohh... did we live?
I think someone brought us inside.
'Bout time you sleepyheads woke up! Come over here.
Get some of this caviar and lobster--they really know how ta treat ya down here!
Yeah, after they electrocute you.
Yeah, what about--ooh, over on this side, please.
Maybe they thought we were bad guys. All is forgiven.
Pretty lavish quarters.
Fitting quarters for the royal guests known as the Fantastic Four.
Yes, your mighty exploits have been heard of down here. Your adventures are nearly as famous as mine.
Nearly. Welcome to my kingdom.
All stand before his highness,
PRINCE NAMOR!

Namor? You're the legendary Sub-Mariner that sailors speak of?
I have been called that.
We never heard of ya in Brooklyn.
Good. You are the first since my own father to discover this ancient world.
I knew if anyone found us, it would be the Fantastic Four.
A great day indeed, that the lovely Susan Storm would grace our shoals.
Oh... um...well, hi.
Prince Namor, we hope to learn about your realm.
Of course, who wouldn't? Don your helmets and come with me.
Atlantis predates your oldest country. Our ancestors left the barbaric surface world and used their advancements to adapt to life under the sea.

My father was an adventurer from the Kingdom of Vermont--
--Kingdom of--?
Shh.
--who found my mother and fell in love. A widowed queen, she gave him the ability to live undersea and they married. On one of his trips back to the surface, he was murdered by traitors-- who wanted to find Atlantis and plunder our treasures!
Soon after, I was born.
HOORAH!
The combination of long-separated bloodlines resulted in my incredible might. In the ocean, my own strength rivals that of The Mighty Thing.
Yeah, right!
The empire had fallen in disarray under the rule of usurpers. Upon adulthood, I drove them out and rebuilt Atlantis to its former greatness.
The Avenging Son!
Over there-- our armada of warships.
Thank you for this tour, Prince Namor. We look forward to showing you some of the wonders of our home as well.
This is your home now, Richards.
Think I got a minnow in my ear--what did you say?

The location of Atlantis is too precious to reveal. You are welcome to become amphibian and stay with us. You may never leave again.
Back, brute!
Yer outta yer fishbrain!
We can't go home?
Let's just calm down...
Yeah, he can calm down first.
KRUNCH
We promise tha--
Now hold on! We have no intention of revealing your location.
You are a surface dweller. The secret is too great to trust with you.

Your father was a surface man...
He made the ultimate sacrifice for his adopted home! I do not think any of you would do the same.
Listen, Prince, why don't--
That's enough!
We're going HOME!
Namor's word is law in Atlantis!
Imperius Rex!
I'll wrecks ya!
Ben! Stomach!
I'd prefer a jaw shot, but if you insist--
WHUMP

My wrath wi--
Thanks, I didn't want him to get a breath.
Johnny, steer us over to that open ship.
Cool!
We are *in there.*
Good, let's get that door closed.
Reed, make this thing go!
Okay, but I think we could have--
Hurry, please, back-up is on the way.
Now--take us out of here.
Since when is Sue in charge?
Since, oh... we got back from outer space.

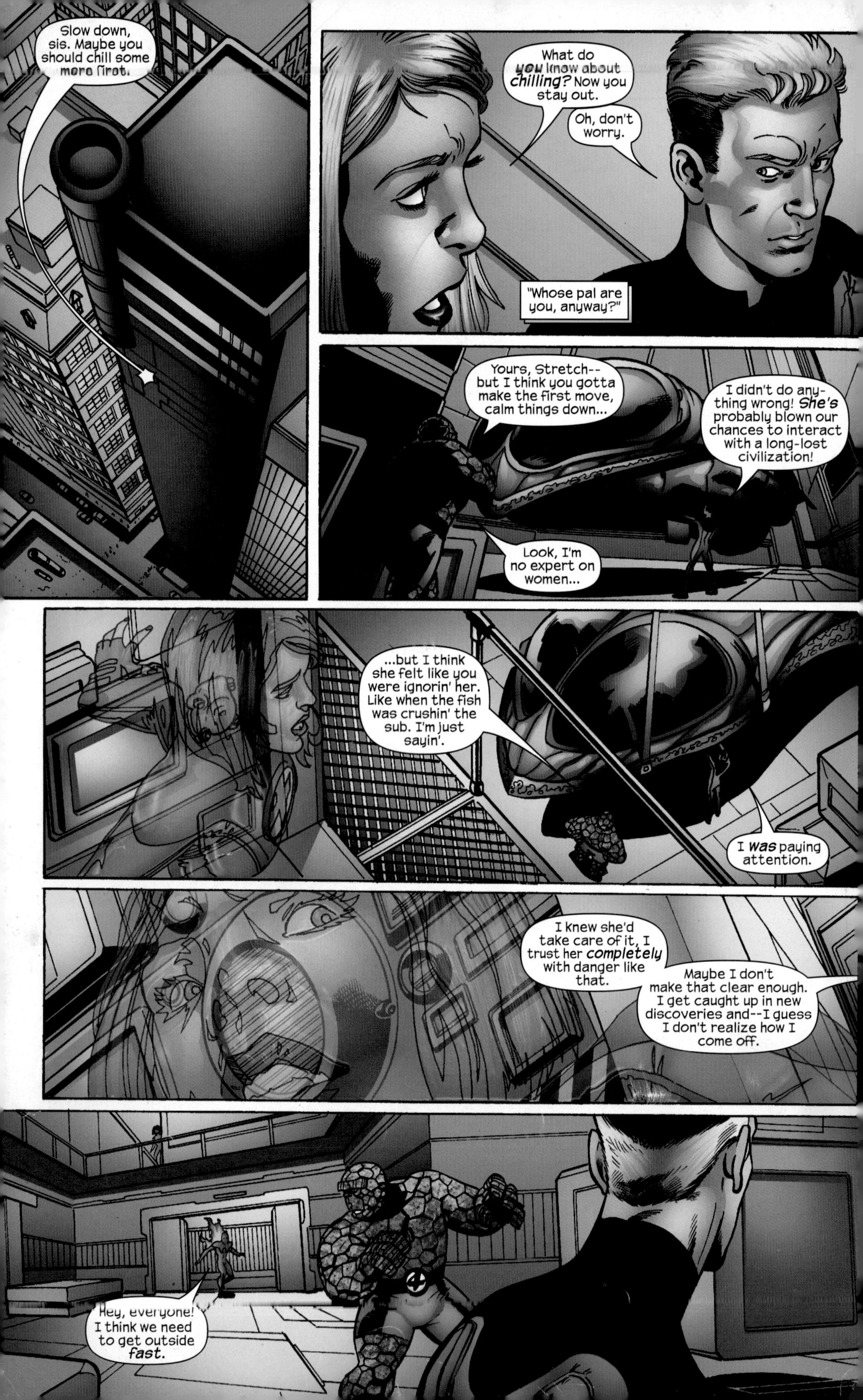
Slow down, sis. Maybe you should chill some more first.
What do you know about chilling? Now you stay out.
Oh, don't worry.
"Whose pal are you, anyway?"
Yours, Stretch-- but I think you gotta make the first move, calm things down...
I didn't do anything wrong! She's probably blown our chances to interact with a long-lost civilization!
Look, I'm no expert on women...
...but I think she felt like you were ignorin' her. Like when the fish was crushin' the sub. I'm just sayin'.
I was paying attention.
I knew she'd take care of it, I trust her completely with danger like that.
Maybe I don't make that clear enough. I get caught up in new discoveries and--I guess I don't realize how I come off.
Hey, everyone! I think we need to get outside fast.

"Atlantis has just invaded New York!"
Citizens of the Sun. I am Namor, Ruler of Atlantis.
Scourge of the Seven Seas.
I have come to your parched and backward world to proclaim my love for Susan Storm!

...what?
WHAT?
So much for the secret city. This is uncomfortable.
This happened a lot when we were in high school.
Susan Storm dared to attack the Monarch of the Depths! She bested my warriors and escaped our realm in one of my very own royal warships!
Such a fiery spirit... such unrivaled beauty... only she is fit to rule Atlantis with me.
Your net has ensnared my mighty heart, Susan.
Will you be my Princess?
Ohh!
Gasp!

Okay, Namor, you're out of line.
Oooooh!
I see you have forgotten my title, Richards.
And you should use mine-- Doctor. A title I earned instead of being born into.
I assume you think you have earned the love of Susan as well?
If you're asking if I'll fight for her, you bet.
Whoa, whoa, you two need to--
Touch me and you seal your fate, Richards.
TOUCH
Stop!
STOP!

Now you're in my territory, boys. You're going back to Atlantis with smoking underpants!
AHHH!
Blast, Richards! Stay solid so you can feel the wrath of Namor!
I'll be glad to...
...your "highness"!
Did--did Reed just make a joke?
Ha ha, take that, fishfa-- wha' hey, he can fly!!

In fact, my future brother-in-law...
--I'm not flying so much as swimming through the air.
A feat which I can do wherever there is sufficient moisture in the air.
Well, whoopty-doo.
Looks like ya got a really hard head, too.
Now what was that about yer power rivalin' mine?
Our liege needs our aid! Please release us, Princess Susan!
Stop saying that! This is so *weird!*
Don't conk out on me yet, I'm just gettin' started.
Worry not! My fine senses detect what I need.

Here. A water source. And for me...
...a power source!
This will also serve another end...
...to take young Jonathan out of the battle.
Sput!
Susan would never forgive me if you were to be hurt.

A question, Namor...
Do you ever shut up?
You go on about how Atlantis is a treasured secret, but all you've done up here is blab about it and yourself.
SLAM
It was going to get out now anyway, so it will be on my terms!
We didn't tell, you hardhead! But you *had* to bring in your forces--you're an Invader!
I would never harm the homeland of my bride!
She's NOT your BRIDE!
Girl, that man's a king or something! You need to marry him!
She's s'posed to leave a doctor for some fool from Atlanta? Nuh-uh!
This is your fault for being so adorable!
I've got to stop it.

If I free you, will you help me stop the fight so I can talk to them?
Anything for our Princess!
Sigh
What--?
Who dares?
This fight is over! We're going to resolve this like adults.
I'm the one who decides my future.
I didn't mean to make it sound like you're my property, Sue. I just...I got jealous.
You're not happy with him! I could tell that when you were in my kingdom.

Even the happiest couples don't get along all the time, Namor. I have to admit, I was being jealous too.
Reed has a love of knowledge and discovery--it's his passion. It bothers me because sometimes *I* want his only passion to be ***me.***
But then he wouldn't be the driven, idealistic guy I was attracted to.
Just like your other passion will always be your home.
While I am flattered, I think you want me for the sake of Atlantis.
Whereas Reed...he wants me for ***me.***
Thank you, Namor.
But I'm staying here with him.
Such wisdom. I knew I'd picked the perfect mate.
I respect your decision.

Truly Susan would only love an honorable man... I will trust your vow of keeping Atlantis' location secret.
In fact, I could help hide your world even better.
Farewell, Susan. Should you ever change your mind, or if Richards is slain in battle, you have but to call for me.
Thank you, my Prince.
Back to the sea...the only place big enough ta hold that ego.
No regrets?
None.
Well, I have one.
"I kind of thought I was going to end up with a hot mermaid girlfriend out of all this somehow."
"Little brother, you're such a romantic."
The End